Robert

and the
Clickety-clackety
Teeth

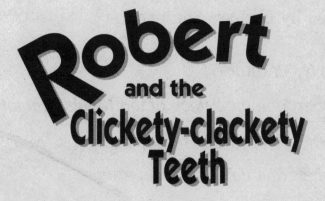

Also by Barbara Seuling

Robert

and the
Clickety-clackety
Teeth

by Barbara Seuling
Illustrated by Paul Brewer

A
LITTLE APPLE
PAPERBACK

SCHOLASTIC INC.

New York Toronto London Auckland Sydney
Mexico City New Delhi Hong Kong Buenos Aires

ISBN 0-439-44376-8

12 11 10 9 8 7 6 5 4 3 2   3 4 5 6 7 8/0

Printed in the U.S.A.   40
First Scholastic printing, February 2003

Contents

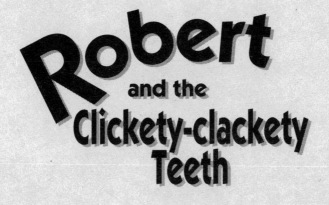

Robert
and the
Clickety-clackety
Teeth

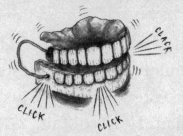

Clickety-clackety Teeth

T ap, tap, tap! Mrs. Bernthal was using her ruler to get the class's attention. "This is the last day to give your presidents' reports. We have several presidents to do, children, so settle down."

Robert and his best friend, Paul Felcher, had spent every day that week after school at Paul's house working on their presidents' projects. Robert had chosen George Washington as his president. He had made a wig out of a piece of white cloth and some rolled-up paper.

1

Robert was next. He waited for the class to get quiet. They were still laughing because Lester Willis had just told them that William Howard Taft, 27th president of the United States, weighed 300 pounds and once got stuck in the White House bathtub. Lester had padded himself with pillows to look extra large, like President Taft.

Robert put the wig over his head. The class started laughing again, but Robert began talking, anyway.

"George Washington was a great general who helped win the Revolutionary War," he said. "He was the first president. Once he chopped down his father's favorite cherry tree. When his father asked if he did it, he confessed, saying, 'I cannot tell a lie.' Some people say that story isn't true, but George Washington was the president, so I think it was."

Then Robert placed a set of plastic false teeth on the table and let them go. The teeth started chattering, *clickety-clack, clickety-clack*. Everyone laughed again, especially Vanessa Nicolini. She giggled so much she started to hiccup.

Robert continued his talk. "George Washington wore false teeth. Some were made of rhinoceros tusks. Some were made of wood."

"Wood?" shouted Lester Willis. Lester always called out. "How come he didn't get a splinter when he ate?"

"Lester, let Robert finish," said Mrs. Bernthal, giving Lester a sharp look.

"None of the false teeth fit," Robert said. "His mouth hurt all the time. That's why you never see a picture of George Washington smiling."

"Thank you, Robert," said Mrs. Bernthal. "That was an interesting report, although you might have talked more about what George Washington did as president than about his teeth. Still, being truthful was a good character trait for a president to have, to set an example, so that story was a good choice."

Robert nodded, the paper curls bouncing. He pulled off the wig as he sat down.

"Susanne Lee, let's hear your report," said Mrs. Bernthal. Susanne Lee Rodgers wore a silver running suit with silver sneakers.

"Which president are you?" asked Mrs. Bernthal.

"My president is me," said Susanne Lee. The children gasped. "When I grow up, I will be the first woman president."

While Susanne Lee was giving her report, Robert thought about having her as president. It made his teeth grind to think about how bossy she would be.

Emily Asher went next. "Abraham Lincoln freed the slaves, who had been brought from Africa against their will," she said. She showed a diorama she had made of Abraham Lincoln's log cabin. Robert liked the tiny ax next to the little pile of logs in the yard outside the cabin.

The kids loved Paul's report. "My president is John F. Kennedy," he said. "President Kennedy said, 'Ask not what your country can do for you. Ask what you can do for your country.'"

Robert had helped Paul rehearse his quotation all week long. Paul said it without one mistake.

Then Paul showed his drawings. "This is John F. Kennedy when he was in the Navy and his PT boat was attacked." The picture showed the boat under fire. He showed the next picture. "And this one is President Kennedy at his desk in the Oval Office." The picture showed a man in a suit at a desk, with the American flag behind him. "And this one is the Kennedy Space Center in Florida." The picture showed a rocket just launched.

"Wow!" said Joey Rizzo.

"Awesome," said Abby Ranko.

"That last picture is not John F. Kennedy," said Susanne Lee. "You just wanted to draw another spaceship." Everyone knew spaceships were Paul's favorite subject.

Paul shrugged. "Well, the Kennedy Space Center is named after him," he said.

When Paul returned to his seat, Robert leaned over and whispered to him. "Don't worry," he said. "When Susanne Lee runs for president, we won't vote for her."

The Long Weekend

T he whole class was outside on the playground after lunch. Nobody was playing. Everyone was buzzing about what they would do over the long Presidents' Day weekend.

"My parents are taking me to the Liberty Science Museum," said Susanne Lee Rodgers. "It's educational."

Robert rolled his eyes at Paul.

"I'm having a sleepover at my cousin's house," said Vanessa.

Lester joined in. "My dad is working Monday. He says there are no days off in trash removal," said Lester. "But he said I could go along on his route with him."

"Maybe it will snow," said Andy Liskin. "Then I can use my new sled."

"We're going to Vermont," said Paul. "It always snows in Vermont."

"No kidding?" said Andy.

"No kidding," said Paul. "My parents are renting a ski cabin for the weekend." He turned to Robert and smiled. "And Robert is coming with us."

"You guys are lucky," said Andy.

"I know," said Robert. He had never been to Vermont, but Paul had told him how great it was. It would be the first time Robert had ever gone anywhere with Paul's family. And there was plenty of snow.

When they came back in from lunch, Mrs. Bernthal gave them work to do in their math workbooks, but it wasn't for long.

"I know you are all excited about the long weekend," she said. "And since you all did such wonderful work on your presidents, we will read another chapter of *Shiloh* this afternoon."

She took out the book she had started earlier in the week. It was about a dog named Shiloh, who was rescued from his mean owner by a boy who was about Robert's age. Robert loved that story, but he almost had to cover his ears when Mrs. Bernthal read the parts where the dog was mistreated.

When the chapter was over, Mrs. Bernthal closed the book and asked them to spend the rest of the afternoon cleaning out their desks.

"Take home or throw out anything from your desks and the coat closet that belongs to you. Over the long weekend the room will be thoroughly cleaned, and anything left behind will be thrown out."

"What about Sally?" asked Robert. Sally was the class pet, a two-foot-long green ribbon snake. Mrs. Bernthal had given Sally to them for being the best class in the school. Robert loved her. He was the Snake Monitor who took care of her.

"Sally will be all right for three days," said Mrs. Bernthal. "I'm talking about papers and artwork and sweaters and anything you have here that should go home."

Children bustled about cleaning out their desks, which were actually long tables with spaces underneath for their books to slide in. Robert found two drawings, a broken pencil, and an empty M&M's wrapper. After Robert cleaned out his things, he went to the back of the room to say goodbye to Sally.

He lifted the lid off the tank to stroke her lightly on her pretty green back. She made an "S" curve when he did that. Robert had fed her that morning, and there was fresh water in her dish. He replaced the lid on the tank.

"I'll be gone for three days," he told her. "I hope you won't be too lonely." Maybe when they came back he would ask Mrs. Bernthal if they could get another snake someday to keep Sally company. He would help pay for it. Sometimes he earned money taking care of people's pets.

When the bell rang and they were dismissed, Robert and Paul ran out of the school and all the way home without stopping once.

Just in Case

"**D**id you pack your heavy mittens?" asked Robert's mom the next morning. "You'll need them when you're skiing."

"Skiing?" Charlie had had his head in the fridge, as usual. He pulled it out when he heard their mom mention skiing. "Since when are you into sports?" he asked Robert.

"It's not sports," Robert said, wishing Charlie wasn't there right then. "It's just . . . just . . ."

"Skiing. It's a sport. Look it up." Charlie loved to tease Robert because he was such a jock and Robert wasn't. "I bet you didn't even know there are left and right skis."

"I did, too," said Robert, fibbing.

Charlie grinned as he pulled out a carton of apple juice and was about to gulp it down.

"Don't drink from the carton," said Mrs. Dorfman. Charlie sighed and poured the juice into a glass.

"Athletic ability isn't everything," Mrs. Dorfman continued. She frowned at Charlie. "Robert has other important qualities." Robert wished she would say what they were, because he didn't know.

"You're really going skiing?" asked Charlie. "Skiing is high up on a mountain. Aren't you afraid of heights?" It was true. Robert remembered once when he couldn't climb a ladder to rescue a cat. After the fourth rung he got woozy. "I'm not afraid," he said, fibbing again.

Charlie wouldn't give up. "And what about the waxing? You know you have to wax skis before you use them, don't you?" He gulped down his juice and put the empty glass on the counter. Robert had never heard about this. It could be another of Charlie's tricks. But before he had a chance to say anything, Charlie left.

Robert ran up the stairs two at a time to get his backpack. He tossed in a Weird & Wacky fact book for the long car ride and picked up the clickety-clackety teeth that were sitting on his desk. He made them move as he talked.

"Hello. I am George Washington. I don't know where the rest of me is. All I found so far was my teeth." He laughed as he tossed the teeth into his backpack and zipped it up. He and Paul could have some fun with them.

It was almost nine o'clock, time for the Felchers to pick him up. He grabbed his backpack and thumped down the stairs again to wait. As he listened for the car, he wondered if Charlie could be right about the wax.

He went into the kitchen and opened the cabinet under the sink. He took out the lemon wax polish and shook it. There was just a tiny bit left in the can. He tossed it into his backpack, just in case.

Snow!

Mr. Felcher stopped the car outside a log cabin. It was snowing lightly.

"Hey!" said Robert, getting out after Paul. "That looks just like the log cabin Emily made for her Abraham Lincoln diorama!"

"Yeah," said Paul. He bent down and scooped up some of the snow surrounding them.

Without a word, Robert fell down into it and made a snow angel by flapping his arms up and down. Nick, Paul's little brother, saw him and did the same thing.

Soon there were three snow angels when Paul joined them, laughing.

Paul's parents unloaded the station wagon and carried some bags into the cabin. The boys carried their own backpacks. Nick carried a snowball into the house.

"You guys sleep up in the loft," said Paul's mom, talking to Paul and Robert while she removed the snowball from Nick's hand.

"Yay!" yelled Paul, running up the stairs. Robert followed him.

The loft was a big open room with a guardrail overlooking the room below. They dropped their packs and fell onto their beds, staring at the slanted ceiling above them. In the ceiling was a skylight.

"This is neat!" said Robert.

Before they had a chance to think, Mrs. Felcher called up to them. "Let's go, boys. We can get in a few hours on the slopes."

Wow. Paul's parents didn't waste any time. Before Robert knew it, they were at Big Bear Mountain's ski shop. Paul and Robert had to rent their skis. Mr. and Mrs. Felcher had their own.

"Paul is still growing," Mrs. Felcher explained to Robert. "We would have to buy a new pair every year." That made sense. Robert had no idea you got skis according to how tall you were. Charlie probably knew that, too.

While Mr. Felcher stayed with the boys, Mrs. Felcher went off to deposit Nick in the day-care center, where parents could leave their toddlers while they were skiing.

"Come on, boys," said Mr. Felcher. "We're next." The attendant measured Paul and Robert and picked a pair of skis and a set of poles for each of them. They exchanged their shoes for heavy ski boots and brought the gear over to a bench.

"I'll go get our lift passes," said Mr. Felcher. "Meet me over at the ski lift when you're ready."

Robert put on the boots. He got up and walked around stiffly. "I feel like the Frankenstein monster," he said.

"That's okay. You look like him, too," said Paul.

Robert sat down again and remembered the lemon wax, which he had stuck in his jacket pocket. He took it out.

"What's that for?" asked Paul.

"To wax my skis," answered Robert.

"You don't use that stuff," said Paul with a laugh. "You use little pieces of hard wax if you need it. But these skis are the kind that don't need wax."

"Oh," said Robert. He tossed the can into the trash bin. It was almost empty. No use carrying it around. At least Charlie wasn't teasing him about the wax. He just never knew with Charlie.

After Paul showed Robert how to snap on his skis, they walked to the ski lift area. It took all of Robert's concentration not to cross one ski over the other. He stared at the long sticks on his feet and wondered when it would feel like fun.

When he looked up, they were in the line for the ski lift. Paul's parents were waiting for them.

"Here, boys, take these," said Mr. Felcher, handing each of them a walkie-talkie. "Call to let us know where you are whenever you change locations."

"Okay, Dad," said Paul. He put his walkie-talkie in a deep pocket of his ski jacket. Robert did the same with his.

A walkie-talkie! Robert thought about what fun that could be.

"And don't play with it," said Paul's dad, as though he were reading Robert's mind. "It's not a toy."

Oops! There went that idea.

"Okay, Dad," said Paul.

As they moved ahead in line, Robert looked up. A huge snow-covered mountain rose before them. Oh, no! This was the part he dreaded.

On the Slopes

Like a big mechanical toy, chairs came around on a kind of belt to pick up skiers and take them to the top of the mountain. It never stopped. It moved slowly, and you had to stand in place and wait for the chair to come up behind you, then sit as it scooped you up, skis and all.

Robert stood next to Paul, feeling his stomach tighten. Paul was cool, but he had done this before. Robert didn't want to disappoint him. He did everything Paul did, except breathe. He couldn't do that until he was on his way.

Zoooop! He was in the chair, next to Paul, being carried up the mountain. He felt his stomach leave when he looked down and saw those two big sticks on his feet and nothing but the snowy mountain below. The only thing holding them in was a thin little bar across their laps. It made him slightly dizzy.

Getting off the lift looked even scarier. He would have to jump off while the chair kept moving. The ground looked very far away.

"We're not going all the way up the mountain," said Paul. "We get off at the bunny slope. That's the one for beginners."

"Okay," said Robert, relieved. He watched Paul and followed his every move. Paul jumped off and glided to the side quickly,

away from the lift. Robert jumped off right after him and did the same.

"You did great," said Paul.

"Really?"

"Really," said Paul.

"But my stomach is still on the chair lift," said Robert.

Paul laughed. "So you didn't like the ride?" asked Paul.

"I cannot tell a lie," said Robert, quoting George Washington again. "I'd rather have Susanne Lee Rodgers help me with my math."

This cracked them up. Now that the lift ride was over, Robert started to enjoy himself. He wasn't coordinated enough to go very far without falling. Paul showed him how to fall and get up, using the poles.

"I never thought I'd have to learn how to fall," said Robert, laughing.

Paul showed him how to zig and zag to move, and how to snowplow, bringing the toes of the skis together to stop. He even learned to do the herringbone, to walk uphill with his skis pointing outward without sliding backward.

When Robert finally got a chance to glide across the snow it felt really nice. He could imagine how those downhill skiers must feel when they came flying down those humongous mountains.

After a couple of hours, the walkie-talkie buzzed, and Paul answered. He made a face.

"What's the matter?" asked Robert.

"There's a lot of static, and . . . wait . . . someone else is talking over my mom's voice."

Robert watched in awe. Wow! You could hear other people's conversations on the walkie-talkies? They could play a great spy game! Then he remembered what Mr. Felcher had said.

"Mom? Mom?" Paul shouted into the walkie-talkie. He listened and said, "Okay. We'll be there." He put the walkie-talkie back in his pocket.

"I finally got a clear connection. It was my mom. She wants us to meet them at the coffee shop in half an hour," he reported.

Josh

At the coffee shop, they sat at a table next to another family. Robert and Paul ordered hot cocoa. Before long, the grown-ups started chatting about skiing. A boy about their age said, "Hi, I'm Josh Robin."

Robert and Paul introduced themselves. "We're from New Jersey," said Paul. "Where are you from?"

"Here," said Josh.

"You live here all the time?" asked Paul.

Josh laughed. "Yup. I do. We used to live in Connecticut, but we love to ski, so my parents bought a house here."

"Wow," was all Robert could say. "Do you ski a lot?" he asked.

"Well, we all love skiing," said Josh. "I get to ski just about every day in the winter. Snowboarding, too."

"Snowboarding!" said Paul. "I love snowboarding. Maybe we can do it tomorrow. What do you think, Robert?"

"Great!" he said. Robert had been on skateboards. Snowboards must be like them. "So we'll see you again tomorrow?"

"Even sooner than that," said Josh. "I heard my parents ask your parents to come over tonight after dinner for hot, spiced cider."

As they returned their skis to the shop, Paul said, "That Josh sure is lucky to live here all the time."

Robert nodded. "Yeah."

It was hard not to yawn through dinner. Robert was so tired he just wanted to get in bed and gaze out the skylight until he fell asleep.

It was a short drive to Josh's house. They turned in at the mailbox marked "Robin." Although the sky was dark, lights around the house lit up the area. Robert could see woods all around. The boys tumbled out as Josh and a big black Labrador retriever met them.

"A dog!" shouted Robert. "What's his name?"

"Napoleon," said Josh.

Robert, happy to be near any dog, tussled with Napoleon in the snow, and both of them ended up on the ground, rolling around.

Meanwhile, the grown-ups and Nick had gone inside.

Robert threw a few snowballs for Napoleon to catch. Josh and Paul had already pelted each other with snowballs.

Then Josh took them around to the back of the house. A snowmobile sat in a small clearing, with a tarpaulin over it. Josh lifted the cover. The snowmobile was shiny blue.

"This is our family car," said Josh. He had a big grin on his face. Otherwise, Robert might have believed him.

"We can't use it on paved roads and highways," said Josh, "but it's great for getting around on the back roads and in the woods."

Robert and Paul leaned over and inspected the driver's seat, the dashboard, the controls. Robert imagined zipping through the snow in it. He stepped back to admire the shape and design and the runners, which were just like the kind you find on a sled. He looked around.

"Hey! There are animal tracks," he said. "What kind of animals do you have around here?"

Josh smiled. "A few black bears, lots of deer, raccoons . . . and some people say there's a catamount."

"A catamount? What's that?" asked Robert.

"It's a big cat, like a mountain lion. There used to be lots of them here."

Robert laughed. Looking closer at the print, he saw it was probably Napoleon's, but he got a thrill just thinking it might have been a bear's.

"I'm cold," said Josh. "Let's go in." They went inside, shaking off snow in the tiny mudroom where coats were hung and boots and skis lined the walls.

Napoleon was already inside, wolfing down his food.

"Come on in, boys, and sit down," said Mrs. Robin. As they took seats on the floor in front of the blazing fire, she went to the kitchen. Napoleon flopped down between Josh and Robert. The Felchers and Mr. Robin were seated on two matching plaid couches, facing each other. Mr. Robin passed around a bowl of pretzels.

Mrs. Robin came out of the kitchen with a tray filled with steaming mugs of hot cider. The spicy smell of cinnamon and cloves filled the room.

The voices of the grown-ups droned behind them. Robert stared into the fire, feeling Napoleon's thick fur on one side,

sipping the hot cider. He wished he could
go to sleep right here, next to Napoleon, in
front of the fire, with the smell of spices
in the air.

Nick came toddling over with a soggy cookie in his hand to feed to Napoleon. It kind of broke the spell, but the moment was nice while it lasted.

When the visit was over, everyone said good night and talked about meeting again tomorrow on the slopes. When they got home, Robert and Paul were so tired, they went right to bed.

In his bed, Robert gazed up through the skylight window overhead. The stars sparkled like diamonds in the sky. There must have been a gazillion stars—more than Robert had ever seen before.

Half-pipes and Ollies

"**T**his is the best fun I ever had!" Robert shouted to Paul, as he sat in the snow. Once again, he had fallen off his snowboard, but it didn't matter. He was having fun.

Paul was a little better at it. He had done it before.

The snowboarding area was not as high up on the mountain, so they didn't even wait in line for the chair lift. Carrying their rented boards, they simply walked up the slope. That was just fine with Robert. On the way,

Paul used the walkie-talkie to tell his parents where they were.

The snowboarding area had sloping sides and a flat bottom. It looked like half of a very large pipe. People were using their snowboards in all different ways. Some looked like they were surfing, crouched down low on their boards, trying to get the most out of the slope. Others were taking off from the top edge of the pipe, gliding down swiftly and up again on the opposite side. A couple of guys were doing twists and flips.

Paul was trying to wiggle himself to go faster on his board, and then up the side a little and down again. Robert stayed on the flat bottom, but even so, he fell off his board again and again.

He was laughing at his latest tumble when Josh came along.

"Hi, guys!"

"Hi, Josh," said Paul. Robert echoed the same.

Josh was really good. He zigged and zagged across the snow, from one side of the pipe to the other. He did amazing things with his knees, bending, then straightening, then turning to the left or right.

"You're really good," said Robert.

"Thanks," said Josh. "I'm trying to do a higher ollie, but it's really hard."

"What's an ollie?" asked Robert.

"It's making your board jump, or hop, over things," said Josh. "It's what you do with a skateboard when you go up a curb." He demonstrated by jumping about a foot in the air. Robert wondered how he could keep the board on his feet.

"Wow!" said Paul. "How do you get it to do that?"

"You press down on your board and lift yourself up at the same time." He demonstrated, jumping into the air and coming down right next to them.

"That's totally cool!" said Robert.

Josh excused himself. "I want to try my half-pipe." He went up to the top of the crater. He got to the edge and crouched low. With a perfect push off, he went flying down one side, across the flat bottom, and up the other side. He twisted around to come down again, landing gracefully with his board flat on the bottom of the crater.

"I guess that's a half-pipe," said Paul to Robert. He shouted to Josh, "You'll be in the Olympics some day!"

"Yeah!" said Robert. "I bet you'll get a gold medal."

"Well, I don't know about that," said Josh, "but a girl from Vermont did win a gold medal. "

Wasn't it incredible that you could win a gold medal for having such fun? Robert crouched on his board, ready to push off again. Maybe this time he could at least end up on his feet and not on his behind.

Whoosh! Off he went. His arms flew out and he felt for a moment like he was flying. Then *thwump!* Down he came, a little shaky, balancing with his whole body and his flailing arms. He had stayed upright for about one second before he went down in the snow.

"That was better!" shouted Paul. He was ready for his own try. Robert got out of the way to watch.

Paul went down the slope and got a little way up the other side, but when he turned his board to come down, he was wobbly. Still, he didn't fall.

"YAY!" shouted Robert. "That was excellent!" Paul swooshed over to Robert.

"This is so much better than skiing, isn't it?" said Paul.

"Yeah," Robert agreed.

They watched Josh again. This time he

worked on his ollie, trying to get "bigger air," to jump higher than before. Robert wondered how long he'd have to practice to make such a move. A gazillion years, probably.

George Washington's Ghost

Robert and Paul looked down over the railing. Below them, Paul's parents sat at the table, drinking coffee and talking. They had brochures spread out in front of them.

"I have an idea," said Robert, going to his backpack on the bed. He unzipped it and took out the clickety-clackety teeth. "I brought these," he told Paul. "We can have some fun with them."

"Cool!" said Paul. "What are you going to do?"

Robert whispered his idea to Paul so the grown-ups wouldn't hear.

"That's a great idea!" whispered Paul.

"Do you think it's okay to use the walkie-talkies?"

"I'm sure it'll be okay in the house," said Paul. "I'll go get them."

"Bring some string, too," said Robert. Paul went downstairs.

"If you're looking for snacks, there are some chips in the kitchen," called Paul's mom.

"Thanks, Mom," said Paul. Robert watched Paul take the chips. Good move! Now he wouldn't look suspicious.

Upstairs, Robert tied the string carefully to the fake teeth so they would still open and close. When Paul came back with the walkie-talkies, he gave one to Robert and went downstairs with the other one. Robert watched from the railing.

Paul went over to Mrs. Felcher at the table. "Mom," he said, "there's someone trying to reach you on the walkie-talkie." He handed it to her.

Mrs. Felcher looked a little puzzled, but turned on the walkie-talkie.

Upstairs, Robert could hardly keep from laughing as he held the string in one hand and the walkie-talkie in the other.

"This is George Washington," he said in a creaky voice into the walkie-talkie. "I am a ghost. I am looking for my missing teeth."

"Do I understand you correctly?" asked Mrs. Felcher. "You are George Washington's ghost, and you lost your teeth?"

Robert dangled the teeth right over Mr. and Mrs. Felcher's heads.

"Ah!" said Mrs. Felcher. "Well, I think we found them."

"Hmmm," said Mr. Felcher. "Isn't it interesting that George Washington knows how

to use a walkie-talkie?" He looked at Paul
as though he would burst out laughing,
but he didn't.

Paul stayed cool as Mrs. Felcher continued to play along. "Well, Mr. President,"

she said, "we'll be sure to leave them here on the table for you."

Robert said, creaking it out, "Okay. I mean, thank you." He shut off the walkie-talkie.

Mrs. Felcher handed Paul the walkie-talkie, and he ran back upstairs. Robert pulled up the teeth. The boys started to laugh and couldn't stop. Downstairs, the Felchers joined in.

"We'll try for another morning on the slopes," Mrs. Felcher called up to them. "Better get some sleep now."

"Okay," said Paul.

They were under the covers, still talking about the ghost teeth performance and what it would be like to live in Vermont and have your own snowmobile.

Robert dreamed that night of winning a gold medal for his snowboarding. Mrs. Bernthal was the one who hung the medal around his neck.

The Worst Thing That Could Ever Happen

It was their last day. Everyone was up early and out on the mountain before the crowds arrived.

Robert and Paul went back to the snowboarding area. Robert got the hang of coming down a small slope without falling. Maybe, with more practice, he'd be able to flip himself into the air the way Josh did.

Halfway through the morning, their fingers were numb. "Maybe we need to go inside and get warm for a few minutes," Paul said.

"Okay," said Robert.

Paul took out his walkie-talkie and tried to get his mom. He listened for a while and didn't say anything.

"What's the matter?" asked Robert.

"It's another bad connection. My mom is talking to someone. I think it's Josh's mom. They're talking about seeing a real estate broker this afternoon."

"Don't real estate brokers sell houses?" asked Robert.

"Yes," said Paul.

Finally, Paul said, "Mom? It's Paul. We're going inside to get warm." He didn't look happy as he clicked off.

He stared at Robert. "I think they're buying a house."

"You mean . . . ?"

"If they're buying a house, we'll have to move."

Robert couldn't believe his ears.

Too stunned to think anymore about snowboarding, they returned their equipment to the rental shop and put on their shoes.

"We're meeting my parents here," said Paul, slumping down on a bench against the wall. "We're leaving early so they can make an important stop before we go home."

That didn't sound good. Robert sat down next to him. He tried to think of something to say that would make Paul feel better. Paul always did that for him when things looked bad. But this was the worst thing that could ever happen. He couldn't think of anything to say.

The List

Sure enough, the Felchers drove up in front of a real estate office.

"We'll only be a few minutes," said Mrs. Felcher. "But come into the building. It's too cold to stay in the car." She unbuckled Nick from his car seat and carried him inside. Mr. Felcher was at her side.

Robert and Paul waited in an outside office while Paul's parents went into another room with a woman who worked there.

"You would get to go snowboarding every day," said Robert, after a short silence. He picked up a flyer showing a man up in the air on a snowboard.

"I know. But I don't want to move."

"You would probably have new friends, like Josh."

"Josh is great, but you're my best friend."

"What'll we do?" asked Robert.

"I don't know," said Paul.

"We have to tell them how we feel. They can't do this," said Robert.

After another short silence, Paul cried, "I have an idea!"

"What?" asked Robert.

"We'll make a list of all the reasons why it's wrong to leave River Edge," he said. "Maybe they'll listen."

"What would we put on the list?" asked Robert. He felt a tiny bit hopeful.

"How about River Edge has Van Saun Park. It's a great park with a zoo and a pond and a lot of ducks. It's a good place for riding bikes."

"That's good," said Robert. "Also, we love our school, especially our teacher, Mrs. Bernthal."

Paul nodded. "That's a good one."

"We'll just have to remember," said Robert. "You remember the park. I'll remember the school."

Paul nodded. "We should include reasons for the grown-ups, too," he added.

"Like what?" asked Robert.

"Well, like things they can do instead of skiing."

"That's good," said Robert. "We can both remember that one."

Mr. and Mrs. Felcher came out of the office smiling and chatting cheerfully with the woman, thanking her. Robert hoped they were not too late.

Home Again

They went back to the cabin and loaded up the car to go home. The Felchers never mentioned moving. While they drove, they listened to CDs. Nick fell fast asleep in his car seat. Robert and Paul rode in silence.

"Are you boys okay?" asked Mrs. Felcher.

"Mom?" said Paul.

"Yes, Paul. What is it?" said Mrs. Felcher.

"Um . . . are you buying a house?"

Robert felt his stomach tighten as Paul asked the question.

Mrs. Felcher turned as far as she could to look at him. "We are thinking about it. Why?"

"Well . . . Robert and I are against it."

Mrs. Felcher looked surprised. "Why?"

"We made up a list," said Paul. "It's all the reasons why you shouldn't do it."

"Let's hear the reasons," said Mr. Felcher. He glanced at Mrs. Felcher.

Paul started. "River Edge has a great park with a zoo and everything. We ride our bikes there."

Robert went next. "We love our school and especially our teacher, Mrs. Bernthal."

"Although there is no skiing, there's a skating rink and a bowling alley nearby and lots of stuff to do," Paul continued.

Robert couldn't help adding another. "Paul and I are best friends. We might never see each other again if you move away."

"Move away?" repeated Mrs. Felcher. She turned as far as her seat belt would let her.

Mr. Felcher laughed.

"It's not funny, Dad," said Paul.

That's just what Robert had been thinking. It was probably the most terrible thing that had ever happened.

"We were waiting to tell you until we found the right house," Mrs. Felcher explained. "It's a vacation house, sweetie. We'll use it for ski weekends and holidays and summers. And Robert can come up with us anytime."

"You mean . . . we'll still live in our house in River Edge?" asked Paul.

"Of course. Why, we wouldn't leave a
great place like River Edge. After all, it's got
a great park and a bowling alley nearby

and an excellent school. And we can't break up such a great friendship." Mrs. Felcher winked at them.

Robert felt like his heart would burst with happiness. Paul shouted, "YES!" and they slapped a high five.

As they got off the highway and drove through their familiar neighborhood, Robert took the plastic teeth out of his backpack. He opened and closed the teeth and spoke in his George Washington voice.

"I cannot tell a lie. I had a great time."

"Well, thank you, Mr. President," said Mrs. Felcher. "You're welcome to join us anytime."

"We loved having you, too, Robert," added Mr. Felcher with a grin.

Paul took the teeth and added his own touch. "Ask not . . . *clickety-clack* . . . what you can do for your country house . . .

clickety-clack . . . but what your country house can do for you."

They all cracked up as they drove into the Dorfmans' driveway.

BARBARA SEULING is a well-known author of fiction and nonfiction books for children, including several books about Robert. She divides her time between New York City and Vermont.

PAUL BREWER likes to draw gross, silly situations, which is why he enjoys working on books about Robert so much. He lives in San Diego, California, with his wife and two daughters.